Published in the US by Nobrow (US) Inc.
Printed in Latvia on FSC® certified paper.

ISBN: 978-1-911171-25-6

Order from www.flyingeyebooks.com

— JOE TODD-STANTON —

THE SECRET OF BLACK ROCK

— FLYING EYE BOOKS —

London | New York

Erin Pike lived with her mum and
her dog Archie near a big fishing town.

She longed to go out to sea, but
it was too dangerous because of...

... the legend of BLACK ROCK!

Every fisherman and fisherwoman had a scary story to tell.

"It never stays in the same place and it could smash a boat to pieces!"

"It's as big as a mountain and as sharp as a swordfish!"

But Erin wasn't scared. Every day she would hide on her mum's fishing boat.

And every day Archie would sniff her out.

At night, she would wait for her mum's safe return...

...hoping she might catch a glimpse of the mysterious Black Rock.

One day, Erin came up with a very smelly plan to outsmart Archie's nose.

Her mum was far too busy to notice Erin was on board.

As the day got later, a fog appeared...

...which got thicker...

...and thicker...

...until Erin couldn't see past the end of her nose.

Suddenly a huge dark shape
loomed right into the boat's path!

The boat turned suddenly,

and as it swept back into the fog...

...Erin disappeared
into the sea unnoticed.

She desperately tried to swim up, but the more she tried, the more she sank...

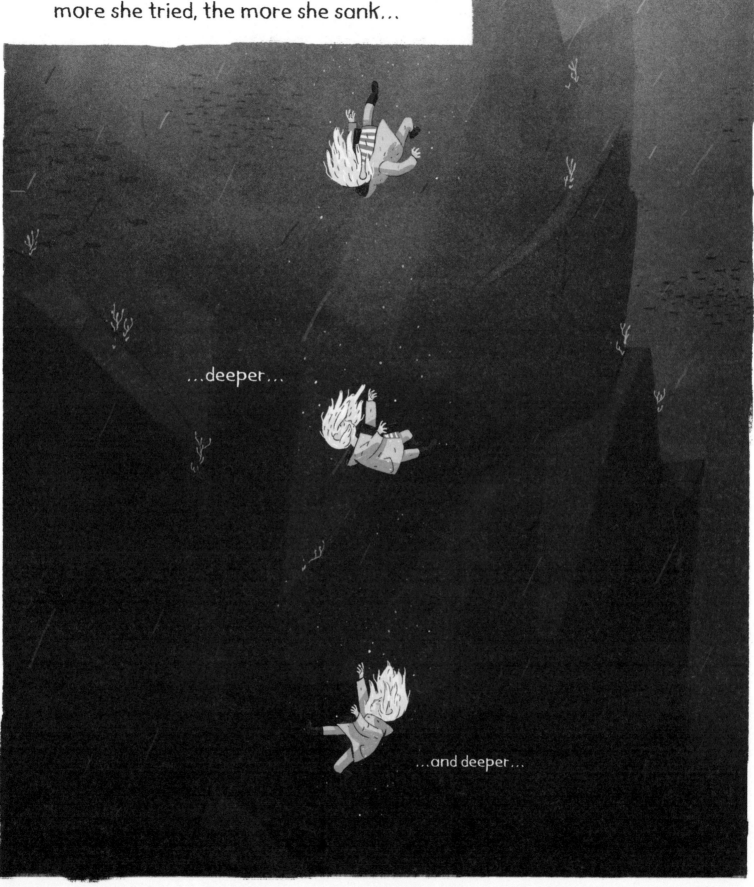

...deeper...

...and deeper...

...until everything went black.
A deep and terrifying rumble echoed around her.

Black Rock woke up!

It picked her up out of the water.
Erin could see that it wasn't just a rock!

It was a huge living creature, surrounded by hundreds of different types of fish.

Jumping back into the water, Erin saw translucent glowing jellyfish...

...huge mustachioed koi carp...

...and anglerfish that had lights just like Erin's lamp!

She could also see scrapes
from lost boats...

...tangled fishing wires...

...and a huge
sharp anchor.

Erin realised she had to tell
everyone the secret of Black Rock.

She picked a fallen rod out of the water, took off
the hook and attached some brightly coloured seaweed.

She cast her line into the sea. The fish followed
the seaweed and Black Rock happily followed the fish...

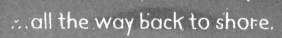

...all the way back to shore.

Back home, Erin tried to explain how Black Rock had saved her, but no one would listen properly.

Later that night, the adults were plotting to destroy Black Rock.
They now believed it was a monster, Erin had to do something!

She rowed out as fast as she could,
but the boats were right behind her!

They had metal claws and drills that
could take the rock apart piece by piece!

As the first claw was about to crash into the rock, Erin jumped
up onto its nose. The whirring and chugging came to a sudden halt!

And as it did, one by one all the creatures that lived on Black Rock swam up to the surface.

In the moonlight, the sea lit up. The fishermen and fisherwomen had never seen such a beautiful sight!

In that moment, they saw how wrong they were. Black Rock wasn't a monster but a home to all these amazing creatures.

After that night the Pikes built a small lighthouse on
Black Rock, so it would always be safe from passing ships.